The Moonbeam Fairies

Caitlin Yannoulatos

Edited by Chantelle Fourie
Illustrated by Bárbarabá

It was time for Mandy to go to bed,

A story my mother told me.

'Sleep tight,
precious one,'
her mommy said.

Down on her pillow went her little head,
But something unexpected happened instead...

TOYS

Up in the night sky the full moon was so bright,
It was as if someone had left on the light.
Through a gap in the curtain the moonlight could stream,
And it placed on Mandy's bed a perfect moonbeam.

Suddenly, giggles and laughter wafted through the air,
It was Moon fairies sliding down the moonbeam looking for fun, not to scare.
Onto Mandy's bed their ride came to an end,
And brought the fairies to a new friend.

Mandy woke and saw two perfect little winged figures,
A mouse could not have been much bigger.
Their friendly faces smiled and greeted,
And on Mandy's bed, Felicity and Daphne got seated.

The three new friends spent time chatting and laughing,
They were having so much fun they didn't even notice the moon had a new covering.
Behind the clouds hid the moon,
There was no way home for the fairies anytime soon...

The fairies worried and their eyes welled up with tears,
But Mandy was calm and settled their fears.
She told them that spending the day with her would be fun,
That they would explore, play, sing, dance and run!

Mandy knew that a new moonbeam would soon appear,
As full moons happened throughout the year.
All they needed was to get some rest,
And the next day together would be their best.

NOTES

Mandy found the perfect bag, tucking the fairies in so they wouldn't be seen.
First, a morning at school filled with learning, chatter, and a trip to the canteen.
The fairies sprinkled some moon dust which made all the food glow,
And decorated all the girls' hair with a pretty bow.

After school Mandy, Felicity and Daphne picked beautiful flowers,
Then, they used stones to build a castle with high towers!
The fairies added lights using their special powers.
They told Mandy about their family and their lives on the moon,
But Mandy sadly realised it was the end of their afternoon.

The sky turned black; the stars started to shine,
A moonbeam landed on Mandy's bed with the perfect design.
It was time for the fairies to say goodbye,
Back home on the moonbeam they needed to fly.

The moonbeam fairies were always special to Mandy, something she would never forget,
Mandy and the long ride from home, something the fairies would never regret.

Felicity and Daphne often rode a moonbeam back to their best friend Mandy,
And they spent many happy years playing, imagining, and eating candy.

An exciting adventure takes an unexpected
turn for Felicity and Daphne.
Can their new friend, Mandy help them find
their way home?